Closing Down Heaven
a novel

Red Deer Pres

Published in Canada by Red Deer Press,
195 Allstate Parkway, Markham, ON L3R 4T8

Published in the United States by Red Deer Press,
311 Washington Street, Brighton, Massachusetts 02135

www.reddeerpress.com   rdp@reddeerpress.com

10 9 8 7 6 5 4 3 2 1

Red Deer Press acknowledges with thanks the Canada Council for the Arts,
and the Ontario Arts Council for their support of our publishing program.

We acknowledge the financial support of the Government of Canada.

Funded by the Government of Canada

 Canada Council   Conseil des arts
for the Arts   du Canada

 ONTARIO ARTS COUNCIL
CONSEIL DES ARTS DE L'ONTARIO
an Ontario government agency
un organisme du gouvernement de l'Ontario

Library and Archives Canada Cataloguing in Publication

Choyce, Lesley, 1951-, author
Closing down heaven / Lesley Choyce.

ISBN 978-0-88995-543-1 (paperback)
I. Title.
PS8555.H668C44 2016   jC813'.54   C2016-905814-X

Publisher Cataloging-in-Publication Data (U.S.)

Names: Choyce, Lesley, 1951- , author.
Title: Closing Down Heaven / author, Lesley Choyce.

Description: Markham, Ontario : Red Deer Press, 2016.
Summary: Author
Ray "16-year-old Hunter has no real purpose [.] until he crashes his bicycle while in the wilderness
and dies. In heaven he meets Archie, a guide who helps him to return to the world. It is only when
Hunter must navigate the hereafter, that he discovers the value of life" - Provided by publisher.

Identifiers: ISBN 978-0-88995-543-1 (paperback)

Subjects: LCSH: Teenagers and death - Juvenile fiction. | Heaven - Juvenile
fiction. | BISAC: YOUNG ADULT FICTION / Fantasy / Contemporary.

Classification: LCC PZ7.1C469Do |DDC 813.6 - dc23

Edited for the Press by Peter Carver
Text and cover design by Tanya Montini
Front cover image courtesy of iStock
Printed in Canada

For Murdo,
Spirit of the West Highlands

WHY I AM TELLING YOU THIS

If I hadn't died
I wouldn't be telling you   this.

I wasn't expecting to die
        but then
                none of us
                ever is.
I wasn't ready for it.
And the odd thing is
I don't think I ever really felt fully alive
until that moment
I died.

WAKING UP IN A NEW PLACE

It was an accident, or so I thought.
But I couldn't remember the details.
When I woke up
I was on some kind of lawn
    that had just been mowed.
You wouldn't expect that

               when you are dead

or maybe you would:
    a mowed lawn
    that you never have to mow.
It was green and sunny
and very nice
and quiet   very quiet.
There were people in the distance
young, old
all colors and types.
Someone was walking toward me
but he was still a   long
              long way off.

I was, of course,
        trying to figure things out.

I couldn't remember
my name, even.   I was trying to
                figure out   if
this was a dream   or real.
But then, I had doubts   all my life
as to what was real and what wasn't.
I wasn't breathing and
when I put my hand on my chest
                I couldn't feel a heartbeat.
                            That was scary
and I started to panic.
That's when   the someone   headed my way
was suddenly
just
there
in front of me.
                Relax
                he said.
                You're
                home.

HOME?

Suddenly
my heart started beating
and I could breathe.
                    Better? he asked.
Yeah, much, I said.
                    Go easy.
                    These things take some
                    adjustment.
Where am I?
He laughed.
                    That's original.
No, really.
                    Really is hard to explain.
Try me.

                    You are where you
                    have always been.
                    This is the real
                    you.
                    You just don't have
                    ... well ...
                    your body.
                    So
                    the good news is
                    you don't
                    have to go
                    to school.

LESLEY CHOYCE

CONTRADICTIONS

But it seemed to me that I did have
a body.
Then what's this? I said
pinching the skin on my wrist.

        That is
        what you want it to be
        for now.
        It gives you a reference point
        of where you fit
        into
        the …   um …   landscape.

How'd I get here?

        Nasty fall.
        Smashed up your bike.

No way.

        Way.
        But
        let's get to that
        later.
        Everything will be explained.
        Everything.

I was still scared
and it seemed
we were playing
some insane   game.

No, it's not a game.
But then
maybe everything   is
all
one big   crazy
game.
Just try to relax
and go with the flow.
So I tried to relax
like he said.
He who?
Who was
this guy?

          I go by Archie.
You read my thoughts?
          No, not exactly.
          It's not like that.
I guessed he was about forty.
He reminded me of someone
I'd seen who acted on
TV shows
someone
familiar like that
who you see in a movie, maybe
and say
Isn't that that guy from ...?
He was wearing an AC/DC T-shirt.
He had a reassuring smile
(which is a good thing to see
when you're dead like me)

and he   seemed
to have all the time
in the world for this.
Whatever *this* was.

What next? I asked.
                    You tell me.
This is all new to me.
I don't know.
Who are you?
                    Well, I'm not God
                    if that's what you were
                    thinking.
Good, I said.
Cause I'm not sure
I believe in God.
                    Good to know
                    we got that out of the way.

Then
having said what I said
I suddenly wondered
if I shouldn't have said it
given my situation
and all.
I swallowed hard.

Is there …?

        A God?

I nodded.

        Well, yes
        and no.

Good to know
we got that
out of the way
I said.

ODD

Yes, it all seemed incredibly

                                       odd.

Archie just stood there, smiling.

                   Take your time.

                   I have …

I know.

All the time in the world.

                   In this world, anyway.

You always speak like that?

                   Like what?

Like you're talking to

a little kid

who doesn't

have a clue.

He suddenly looked hurt.

                   Sorry.

I'm sixteen, I muttered   and then paused.

Was sixteen.

                   Do you remember

                   the accident?

What accident? I began.

But then it started

to come back.

THE WOODS

I was in the woods, yes.
On my bike
my kick-ass, brand new ultralight
ultratight
ultra heavy duty
ultra everything
mountain bike.
I was deep, deep, deep
into the forest of spruce and pine
racing past   lake after lake:
Lake Loon, Long Lake, Rocky Lake,
Stone Throw Pond, Lucky Lake, Trout Lake, Sandy Lake
Final Lake
and when the trail ran out
I just kept going
and going
into the wild, into the land of
rocks and scrub and barren bluffs
and up and down
fast and then faster
and nothing stopping me
breathing hard and harder
leg muscles like iron
arms flexed and brain fueled
with visions of a zero-gravity bike rider.

LESLEY CHOYCE

No, man
I'd never felt like that before.
Never had the balls like this before.
No helmet
always hated wearing one
wind in my face
bike and boy welded as one.
Fearless and free.
The new me.
The daring me.
The fully alive me.

Hah!

Forded a stream
made a rainbow spray
jumped a couple of big rocks
found an impromptu
log bridge

(steady, boy, steady)

then a low granite outcrop
just pedal and leap
and the destination will appear
mid air
and it did—
another flat rocky top just up ahead.
But
I soon realized
I don't have enough air
not enough height
not enough wiggle room between
my bike and planet earth

but I'm a believer, see.
So I try to lift
me and my machine
inches, inches
and I almost   *almost*
had the speed
the height
the distance.

But not enough.
Then

                slam:

Young Man No Match
for Rock Face
the headline could have read.

Do I remember pain?
No.
Do I remember my drop
into the bushes, onto the stones below?
No.
Do I remember dying?
No.   Not at all.

SLEEP

After I remembered the crash
the dying
the whole ill-planned adventure
I must have gone somewhere
in my head
must have   gone to sleep
'cause later I woke up
and I was in this other place
this green sunshine place.

                Welcome back, Archie said.

Where'd I go?

                You remembered.

The accident, yes.

                It was one hell of a ride
                while it lasted.

You can say that again.

                So now you know how
                you ended up here.

How long ago was that?

                It's been a while.

Days?

                Months—
                in their time.

Months?

        Funny, eh?

But where have I been
since then?

        Just taking your time
        waking up
        is all.
        You needed to rest.

Oh, boy.
What about
my mom
and dad?
And everyone?

        Not good.
        Not good at all.

Shit.

        Shit is right. Sorry.
        It was weird
        and, well, not quite
        right.

Why?

        They never found you.

You mean, my body?
My body is still out in the woods?

        And that bike
        you were so proud of.

LESLEY CHOYCE

How?

How is that possible?

        Oh, they tried.

        You were just so far in.

        No one thought you'd be

        way off the trails.

I was stupid.

        We don't make those kinds of judgments

        here.

I'd never done anything like that before.

I had turned a corner. It was the new

me.

I was going to live my life like

that ride from then on.

        It sure as hell must have been great.

So I was punished

for going beyond my

limits?

        No, dude, it doesn't work that way.

        If you have to blame something

        blame gravity.

        But we don't do the blame game here.

But if they never found

my body …?

Well, they searched and searched.
Dogs, hikers, bikers, cops, searchers
helicopters, army, satellite.
But there was a storm a couple of days
after your escapade.
A big one. Lots of trees down. No one
could find you.

But they know I'm ...

Yeah, they came to accept it.
Sort of.
Not the best scenario
but there it is.

Boy Dies in Woods and Is Never Found.

It's just one of those things.

ARCHIE

A long silence in a bright green place.
The pieces starting to fit together.
My brain (do I have a brain?)
beginning to see the thread of events
beginning to accept.
No, not accept.

> Doesn't do much good
> to have regrets
> or fight it.

Another long whack of silence and light.
Who are you, anyway? I asked.
That goofy smile on his face.

> Think of me as your advisor
> your guide.
> Your mentor.
> Everybody needs somebody
> to lean on.

Isn't that a line from a song?

> Traveling Wilburys.

Oh, boy.

> Come on, Hunter
> have a sense of humor.
> It helps.

What did you call me?

          Hunter. It's your name.

          Remember? Hunter Callaghan.

All of a sudden I had a flood of memories.

My mom calling me

to come in from the backyard.

A teacher calling my name

for attendance.

A girl in the sixth grade

whispering my name in my ear.

Who was that girl, anyway?

Why can't I remember her name?

But at least

I now *had* a name.

Hunter.

Hunter Callaghan.

CHOOSE

What do I do now? I asked.

        Pretty much whatever you want.

        Choose when you're ready.

What are the options?

He held out his arms.

        Well, whatever.

        When you don't have a body

        you have a lot more options.

I looked down at my arms and legs.

But I still have a body, I said.

        Yeah, you wanted to hang onto that idea

        for now.

        Most folks do

        until they get adjusted.

I held my hands out in front of me.

This isn't real?

        Here, there's no big deal

        in differentiating between

        what's real and what is not real.

        Didn't you once say that

        yourself

        back in the day?

Guess I did
but I didn't know
what I was talking about.
Damn.
                    Don't worry.
                    You'll get the hang of it
                    after a while.

I looked off into the distance
where I saw that crowd of people moving around.
They seemed to have bodies.
What about them?
                    They wanted to make you feel
                    at home.

Is there a name for this place?
                    Guess.
You want me to say it?
                    Yes.
Am I in heaven?
                    Something like that.
                    Heaven is as good a term
                    as any.
Archie?
                    Hunter?
What are you here to teach me?
                    Whatever you need.
I don't know what I need.
                    That's a good place to start.
                    You're keeping your options open.

FUZZY

Then something happened.
Archie faded.
I faded.
Everything just got misty.
Fuzzy.
I wanted to try to figure things   out.
I'd never really thought
much
about dying.
So now that I was ... um
dead
I had to sort it all   out.

So I went walking in that
fog
thinking
This is
heaven
although
I had never thought much
about heaven.
Truth is
I   thought
when you   are dead
you   are dead
and that was all there was to it.

But this
was
the   afterlife.

I smiled
and the fog cleared
and the sun   came out again
        which all
                seemed
a little   too   Hollywood
to be real.
And the   truth is
it didn't feel   quite right
which is when the fog began to roll back in.
Give me a break
I said   out loud.

THE BODY OF THE DECEASED

I kind of wished I was wearing a watch
so
I could figure out time.
I had clothes   the clothes I wore
when I died:
                    old favorite blue flannel shirt
                    ripped, faded jeans
                    work boots with steel toes.
The clothes made me think of my body
way out there in the boonies
rotting away.
Maybe   someday
some hiker would come along
and find nothing but   my bleached bones
and the steel toes of my old boots.
A little DNA homework and   yes
they'll say
that's what happened to poor old
Hunter Callaghan.
Oh, and the rusty frame of my bike
                    would be there as well.
End of story.
No, not really an ending.

More like a beginning
because what I thought was the end
(last breath, last heartbeat, famous last thought)
was just a phase shift
with   as Archie would say
plenty of options.

So I thought about the fog
and the sun
and how I somehow   did that
                    made that happen
with my mind
(or whatever consciousness was left of me).

But I was feeling homesick
for   … well …   home.
And then someone turned on
the video playback
of chunks of my
life
which went on   for a really long
time.
And I thought that maybe
my short tenure   on planet earth
wasn't as inconsequential
                    as I thought.
Inconsequential?   Insignificant?   Unimportant?
Well, that was the old me
                    or so I thought.

But I had a history teacher once—
                    Mr. Blomquist
fortyish, smart-alecky, bifocaled, bit of a belly
(and a great belly laugh)
who   in describing the Versailles Treaty
              at the end of WWI
said famously
                    Everything
                    has consequences.

I reran the final
sequence   of my life   again:
·mountain bike
crazy great day
ride in the woods
head rush
body rush   and then
              boom.

Boy Leaves Planet
       and Ends Up
              Here.

If I could just figure this out
understand the rules here
learn how to control my thoughts
my emotions
              I might just ...

Just what, idiot?
        I asked myself.

                And then it slammed me.
Yeah, slammed
                just like that asshole piece of
granite
        left there waiting for me by
            some damn glacier.
"Everything has consequences, Hunter."
(Thank you, Mr. Blomquist.)

Might just what? you ask.

Well …

LONELY IN HEAVEN

So, yes
             you can be nostalgic in heaven.
             You can be sad in heaven
             and you can be lonely in heaven.
I wished myself back home
                      and alive
and it didn't work.
So I felt abandoned
             and lonely   again.

That crowd reappeared in the distance
so I started walking
that way.
It was far   far   away   but I thought
Don't I have   all the time   in the world?
And
don't I recognize a face or two   over there?
Even though that seemed
                      unlikely
from this distance.
The boots felt a little tight now.
Do your feet grow in heaven
or are you supposed to just
             chuck your boots
and go barefoot up here?

Okay, I get it.

That crowd   just kept
getting further   and further
away.
          So
                    I
took the hint   unlaced my boots
took off my socks.
(Funny thing   my socks
      were really stinky.)
I'd been dead for   what was it?
                    Months?
And I guess a dead boy's socks
could still   stink
up here
          wherever here was.
Funny, eh?
This place was   so
          full of surprises.

So now my feet were on the grass
and that felt   amazing.
Losing the shoes
was all part
of some kind
of   transition   or
transformation
I suppose.

The crowd looked a bit closer now
and I *really*
wanted   to talk
to someone.   Anyone.
I began
          to run:
barefoot boy on green grass
smiling.
But there was a voice   behind me.
A girl's
voice.
              Hey!   Wait!   she said.
I stopped
turned
saw her.
I didn't know who she was.
Just some random girl
                  in heaven.
She looked scared
          confused
and I now vaguely recognized her—
one of those girls from school
somebody I once knew maybe
before she
got older
and lonelier
and weird.
              Hunter?
              Is that you?

I tried to remember who she was.

  We looked at each other.

  She looked down at my bare feet.

  When she looked up

  I looked   into her eyes.

Oh.

    We were friends   remember?

    Friends in sixth grade.

The voice. Yes.

Of course. Trinity, right?

    Yes. And no.

Huh?

    Hunter, I don't understand.

    What is this place?

Long story.

    How did I get here?

I didn't want to tell her.

    What are *you* doing here?

More news I didn't want to report.

    Can you

    help me?

TRINITY AND ME

I looked over my shoulder
but the crowd   had vanished.
So it was just
       Trinity and me.
How long have you been here? I asked.
               I don't know.
               I think
               I just got here.
Do you remember what happened?
               What do you mean?
Never mind. It's not important.
               But I'm so confused.
Join the club, I wanted to say
but didn't.
Trinity, all I know
is that
it's going to be
okay.
        Okay.

TRINITY ASLEEP

She said she was tired.
I told her to rest

              and she fell asleep.
I tried to remember
why we stopped being "friends."
In junior high she started going out
with an older guy.
I think she then started getting into
drugs.
There were   problems at home

              problems at school

              problems with the boy

              problems with the next boy
and she always looked   unhappy

              angry

              not quite

              right.
Like almost everyone   else
I kept my distance, I guess.
Until
now.

I saw Archie walking our way.
He looked at Trinity

           asleep on the grass.

              Oh, boy, he said.

LESLEY CHOYCE

Oh, boy is right.

                  She found you
                  almost right away.

Why me?

                  You were the one
                  she needed.

We haven't hardly spoken to each other
since …

                  Doesn't matter.

Why is she here?

                  C'mon, dude. We've been
                  down that dusty road.

Why did she find me?

                  Well, that's the interesting part.

What do you mean?

                  I mean
                  she found you
                  because you were the one
                  she needed.

But I don't have a clue about what's going on.
You're my teacher
my mentor
my guide or whatever.

                  Guru.
                  I like to think of myself
                  as your guru.

Okay, guru.
Then explain.
Why me?

Well,
the rules are always changing
here.
Nothing
is static.
Good to see
you ditched your boots.

What do you mean the rules are changing?

Used to be
only old souls
acted as ... um ... guides.
You're *not* an old soul.
You're kind of a
rug rat soul.

I don't know anything about souls—old or young.

Like I said
You are, well,
just young in that department.

Thanks for the news.

Just sayin'.

Archie, if you're my guide, my advisor, then advise
please.

EXPLANATIONS

       Okay, Hunter
       the girl shows up here
       confused
       and she needs someone
       and that someone is you.

But I just got here.

       No, you didn't.

I forgot.

       Forgetting is an important part
       of settling in here.

Great.

       Well, anyway, about the rules.
       I guess they now allow guys like
       you
       to act as advisors
       guides
       gurus
       to someone like her.

Oh, shit.

       Yeah, oh, shit.

Archie looked up at the sky.

       Looks like rain.

It rains here?

Anything can happen.
Used to be things were predictable
but not so much anymore.
I don't get it.

If you don't get it, who does?

Maybe no one.
There are committees of sorts
that try to solve any problems
just to keep things running smoothly
but there are so many
random factors.
Ever study quantum physics?

Sorry, I didn't get that far in high school.

Understood.

Well, now what?
What do I do
when Trinity
wakes up?

Help her
get adjusted.
That's your
job now.

EMPLOYMENT

So now I have a job?
          Sort of.
          Everyone has to
          carry their weight
          eventually.
          In the universe
          there is no
                    free ride
                    free lunch
                    free beer.
There's beer here? Is there a legal drinking age?
          You're dead and you're thinking about beer?
I'm thinking about many things.
Just trying to get a handle.
          You may never
          quite get a grip
          on that handle.
          Like I say
          it's a very fluid   situation.

Archie smiled, stroked his chin
looked like he was about to   laugh.
What do I do
when she
wakes up?
          That's an easy one, dude.
          Take her on   a date.

SHELTER

Truth is
      I'd never been on   a date.
I'd led such a sheltered life.
Sixteen short / long years
of trying to figure out
who I was.   Identity
was always so confusing.

          Hunter Callaghan—
          boy something or
          boy nothing.

My mom said
I hardly ever cried
when I was a baby.   They tested
          my hearing
          my heart
          my head

and said
it was all normal.   I was normal.
My father said   normal's good.
I just seemed to lack

          a spark

like I saw in other kids.

The mountain bike thing
was that spark   finally.
And then
all too soon   the spark
                                              went
                                              out.

Way too soon.

Back on   planet earth
I had often felt   all alone
in the whole freaking
universe.
But now   well
things were different
yet I was still
lost
confused.

Yo, Archie, where'd you go?

FIRST DATE IN HEAVEN

Trinity awoke.
                    Where am I?
Still here
with me.
Do you remember?
She had that look of major confusion.
(Damn, there's a lot
of confusion
here.)
                              Oh, right.
                              Here.
                              Now what?
                              You didn't really answer
                              my questions.
I will.
I promise.
But first
I'm supposed to ask you something.
                    What?
Will you go on a date
with me?
                              A date?
Yeah. With me.
(Was that a smile
or was she about to laugh
at me?)

                    I wasn't going to laugh
                    at you.
You can read my mind?
                    Idiot, I read
                    your face.
Oh.
Well?

                    Yes,
                    I would love to
                    go out with you.
                    What will we do?
(I had once heard the term "divine inspiration"   so
I thought
I'd empty my head
and wait for   it:
divine inspiration.)
                    Well?

We'll go
bowling.
                    Wow.
                    Bowling.

HELL, YES—BOWLING.

I was feeling good.   Trusting my instinct.
                       Trusting my gut.
                       Trusting, yeah,
                       just trusting.
The sun was out.   Trinity looked happier
                       and more beautiful
                       not a trace of hurt
                       or anger
                       as I read
                       her face.
And there it was: an open-air bowling alley.
One lane set up on neatly trimmed grass
bowling balls and pins to knock down.
I let her go first
and then me   and it all seemed
                       so normal
except   of course   the fact that
the pins had a way of setting themselves
back up.
So we bowled for a while
like we'd been doing it   all our
                           lives.
And she said
              I've never, ever been
              this happy.
And I said
Me, too.

     LESLEY CHOYCE

IF YOU CAN BOWL HERE ...

Yeah, if you can bowl here
I wondered what else you could do.
And I guess she read my face again just then.
A big shit-eating smile on my sixteen-year-old face
cause

> she kissed me
> a slam dunk of a kiss.

Wow.

And I wondered if Archie was bullshitting me about not
having a body, that it was all an illusion.

> But then I noticed
> the celestial bowling alley
> was gone.

Trinity noticed, too.
I said
That's the way it works here, I guess.
And this changed   her mood
> her face
> her trust in me.
> Hey, she said
> just where exactly are we, anyway?
> Did you give me some kind
> of drug or something?

Of course not.

IT'S JUST COFFEE

Let's go get a coffee   I ventured.
                    I'm scared.
Me, too.
Or at least I was.
Now
I don't know.
Now that you're here
I'm like
sort of
okay.

That made her smile.
                    Coffee it is.
So we walked until we found a small table by a pond
with a couple of cups of steaming coffee.
There were ducks
in the pond.
We sat down.
                    This is really
                    romantic.
Cool, eh?
                    No boy ever treated me
                    like this.

I guess I blushed.
She reached over
took my hand.

        I wish things could just go on
        like this   forever.
Maybe they will
I wanted to say out loud
but didn't.

        The guys who like me
        mostly treat me
        like dirt.
Those words hit me hard
stabbed me, even.   I felt
her pain   and it was
my pain.

If you could point them out, I said
I'd beat them up.
(She looked around.)
        They're not here.
Nope. Just us.
        What now?
That's a good question.
A really good question.

WHAT TO DO WHEN YOU RUN OUT OF COFFEE

When the coffee was gone
I was expecting refills
or something.
But all I had
was an empty cup.

Instinct was telling me
it was time to move on.
I saw rain clouds on the horizon.
The ducks flew away.
Let's go, I said.

We walked
and it got darker.
And then we were
at school
the old high school.
                        Oh, shit, she said.
I shrugged
and felt the first drops of rain.
We went in
and it smelled
like
the old high school.
No one was around
and it was kind of echoey in the halls.

I hated this place.
Yeah, it had its bad moments.
I think everyone hated me
back here.
That's not true.
Even those boys who said
they liked me.
Who were they?
Caleb.
Yikes.
Ethan.
Ouch.
Jake.
Why did you go out
with such
creeps?
Because.
I decided to leave it at that.

Let's go sit in
the cafeteria, I said.
Okay.
Sure enough   it was empty.
There were   two trays of food
                     at a table
                     with meatloaf
                     and mashed potatoes
                     and canned peas.
And suddenly I was hungry
and so was Trinity.

So we ate in silence
and then   I cleared my throat.

I think I'm supposed to tell you
about all this.
                        All what?
Where we are.
                        Yeah, I guess so.
                        But for now
                        I was hoping we could just
                        be.
Well, okay.
Maybe later.

                No.   Maybe
                you better tell me   now.

Let's start
with my story.
I had a bike accident
and died.
                        I didn't know.
                        When?
March, I think. When I woke up I was
dead.
                        Which means?
You are, too.
Trinity buried her head in her hands and began to cry.
I'm sorry.
I'm sorry.

Maybe I shouldn't have said that.
But Trinity, I said
Archie says
dead isn't exactly dead.
          What does that mean?
          Who's Archie?

Archie's my mentor, my guide, my guru.
(I saw a look of horror on her pretty face.)
          I'm starting to remember.
          I remember how I died.
Do you want to talk about it?
          No.
The good news is …
          Screw the good news.
(I decided to say what I had to say, anyway.)
The good news is
this
is not
so bad.

NOW THAT WE HAVE THAT OUT OF THE WAY

I think I'm supposed to tell you
        Tell me what?
That I'm here for you.
        You're what?
I'm here to act as your guide.
        Why you?
I don't know.
        Then tell me everything
        about this place.
        Where are we, exactly?
        How does it work?
I don't know.
        Great guide you are.
I guess I'm not doing so good.
        Some date!   (she said angrily).
        Freakin' high school cafeteria.
It wasn't my idea.
        Then whose idea was it?
        God's?
Nobody's mentioned him.
There seems to be some
confusion
about who's in charge here.

Archie's been pretty vague.
                    This guy, Archie.
                    Do you trust him?
I think so.
                    Where'd he come from?
I don't know.
I guess he lives here
or works here
or something.

THE SIXTH GRADE

Do you remember the sixth grade? I asked.
                    Yes.
Do you remember whispering my name?
One day in September
                    you were sitting behind me
                    and you said
                    my name.
Do you remember?
             I think so.
That's my only clue.
That's why I'm here
for you.
             Okay.
Okay what?
             Now I'm ready to tell you   how I died.

TRINITY'S STORY

Trinity took a deep breath.
I took a deep breath.
The big empty cafeteria took a deep breath.

> Jake was being cruel to me.
> He said we were through.
> It was really bad timing.
> My mom was in the hospital.
> My dad was away on business.
> School was crap
> and I just wanted it all to
> go away.
> So I drank some of my dad's vodka
> and took some pills   but
> I did not   want to die.
> I repeat   (she now said loudly)
> I did not   want to die.

I was feeling her pain
really feeling it.
Big time.
I was waiting for some insight
to say the right thing.

I wish we had stayed friends, I said.

I'd lost track of you.

It was a big school.

I wasn't exactly Miss Congeniality.

When did this happen?

June 15.

We only had   one more week
of school.

DO THE MATH

I sat silently, holding Trinity's hand.
June 15.
My bike accident had been
in March.
March 21.
First day of spring.
I couldn't have helped her.
In June I was already dead and gone.
Dead and gone   but not buried.
Bones and bike out there in the wild.

So   back in that other world
I was   at least
                                more than two months dead.

Did it matter?
Maybe.
I did not reveal this to Trinity.

Trinity, I said.
                Yes?
Let's be good to each other.
                Okay.   (She squeezed my hand.)
                             And then
                             I kissed her
                             and made the world
                             (that world, this world)
                             go away.

DARKNESS AND THE LIGHT

I woke up   and thought
I'd been dreaming—   thought it might be
all one big   screwy dream.
                Where were you just then? Archie asked.
High school cafeteria.

                Figures. (He sort of laughed, snorted.)
Where is she?

                Hold on. Not yet.
How do I know what's real here
and what's a dream?

                You don't. But
                for the most part
                it doesn't matter.
                It's all the same thing.
                I told you that before.

When are you going to give it to me straight?
When are you gonna stop being so vague about things?
When are you going to tell me who the hell is in charge here?
Who is it, exactly, that is calling the shots?

                Don't get riled at me, cowboy.
                I'm just the messenger.
So give me some clear messages.

                Okay, back to your list.

Thank you.

>A. I'm giving it to you as straight as I can.

>B. It's vague because words/language
>don't quite work to explain things.

>C. No *one* person is really in charge.
>There are these committees. That's
>the only word I can use to describe them.

>D. They don't even call the shots.
>They make suggestions
>and sometimes shit happens.

Well that helps,   (I said sarcastically).
So where is she?

>Trinity?

Yes. And don't tell me she was the Father, Son, and Holy Ghost.
>Good one, doodle.

AIRPLANES

And that's when an airplane flew over.
No way, I said.

>   No. It's not what you would call
>   "real."
>   Just a kind of visual representation
>   a transportation device for
>   travel back and forth.

Back and forth?

>   That's part of what I have to
>   talk to you about.

I didn't come here on some friggin' airplane?

>   No, son.
>   You rode your bike here, remember?

Funny.

>   A sense of humor is a really good thing.
>   Especially now.

Pardon me if I repeat myself
but where is Trinity?

>   Okay, chief.
>   Here goes.

So spit it out, Big Brother
or whoever the hell you are.

Well,
she went
back.

On an airplane?
No, Hunter.
Not really an airplane.
But she's gone.
She's back.
Back where she came from.
Why? How?
How I can't really explain.
But *why?*
Yes, why?
I thought I was
her guide
her guru.

You did okay, buddy.
I'll write up a nice report
on you.
Report?
The committee likes paperwork
likes to keep records and such.
Screw the committee.
Why is she gone?
Okay, like I told you
things are changing here.
It's not like the old days.
Apparently it was decided
that the old version ...

Of heaven?

>Whatever …
>wasn't working that well
>anymore.
>There are some new ideas
>kicking around   but
>nothing is quite settled yet.

So?

>So, they're sending people
>back.
>Most recent arrivals
>go first.
>Trinity just got here
>so it was relatively easy
>to ship her back.

>>A sudden massive wave
>>of loneliness and loss
>>swept over me
>>like a tsunami.

What am I going to do now?

LESLEY CHOYCE

THE SO-CALLED EXPLANATION

Let me spare you the drama
and try to explain what Archie had to say.
He explained that
in the good old days,
folks would arrive and be happy.
Totally satisfied, he said.
Boom, you die. Boom, you wake up and smell the roses.
Ever after.
Many young souls had to go back
for another kick at the can
but old souls could eventually stay on and play shuffleboard
or whatever they wanted
for eternity.

But times change. People change. Heaven had to change.
It wasn't just the overcrowding issue.
It was more than that.
Down on earth
people's *beliefs* had changed
and
as crazy as it sounded
heaven had to keep up
with the times.
There were lots of proposals for a new model but
there was no agreement
so, in the meantime

a lot of
people had to go back to their old lives.
Recent arrivals—especially young souls—
would go first.
Trinity was on the first "flight" out / back.

ARCHIE'S DILEMMA

I'm really going to miss her, I said.

        No you won't.

But I already do.

        Well, here's the thing.

What thing?

        I guess I just need to come right out
        and say it.

It?

        You're next.

Holy shit.

        Holy shit is right.

But I'm dead.
The old me
is rotting out there
beneath what was once
an awesome
off-road bike.

        That's just a corporeal issue.
        Not a big deal.

Seemed like a big deal at the time.

        I'm gonna miss you, champ.

What if I don't want to go?

        Hey, I'm not gonna touch that.
        Then we have to get into the
        whole
        freakin' free will / predestination

bullshit.
We're all sick of that
debate.
So don't go there.

What if I just walk away
right now?
What if I ignore you
and use my will to
make you
go away?

Hey, that's not nice.
You'd do that to me?
Man ...

Well?

Hunter, get serious.
Wouldn't you like to see
your parents?
Wouldn't you like to
slip back into your body?
Wouldn't you like to
see
Trinity
again?

ARCHIE'S LAST STAND

Yes, I said.
I would.
But how
would that work?
                        Trust me.
                        You just have to
                        trust me.
But I don't really know you.
Were you someone I knew
in real life?
                        Yes and no.
Here we go again.
                        Just let me finish
                        what I have to say.
So finish.

                        I'm not sure
                        but I think there are plans
                        for closing down
                        heaven.
All this?
                        All this.

That doesn't make any sense.
                        Well, I'm just saying
                        what I think is happening.
                        Look, buddy boy,

I'm only a tad more informed
than you.

And you call yourself my guru?

Good.

Hang onto that sense of humor.

You'll need it.

Now what?

Say goodbye
to your old pal
Archie.

Goodbye?

COLD

That's what I felt first.
Cold.
Then the pain slammed into me   really hard.
I was on my back   on hard jagged rock
jammed up against a rock face   busted bike tangled
in my arms and legs.   I could taste
blood   dripping from
my forehead   and I was having a hard time
breathing.   It was getting
dark   and I didn't know
what had happened.   I was scared
and didn't think   I could move
but I shoved one arm   up into the air
and it hurt so bad   I screamed out loud.
I tried to heave the bike   off me
but it hurt worse   so I tried to slow down
take my time   breathe deeply
and get my wits.

Then I remembered
what I had been up to.   Fearless me
maybe for the first time   in my entire safe little
life.
But I   went too far.
Did I have broken bones?   Would I live?
I tried to wriggle   tried to wrestle

my way out
and that's when I discovered
This made
No sense at all.
Why was I

of this mess
I had no clothes.
no sense.

naked?

I shivered
Night was coming.
something.
Every cell in my body
ached.
My brain was on fire.
My lungs hurt.
My legs hurt.
My arms barely worked.
But I had no

and screamed a second time.
I had to do

choice.

SALVATION

I climbed up finally onto the rock
where I'd launched my bike from
and stood there looking at the rising moon.
Naked Boy in March on a Boulder in the Middle of Nowhere.
Something about this photograph was not quite right.
Hadn't I just been
somewhere else?

Brain injury, I figured. Memory not quite right.
But where the hell were my clothes?

        Forget about your clothes.
        Be happy to be alive.

Who said that?

        It's me, your inner voice.

But I'm gonna die here.
I'm hurt.
I'm freezing.

        I know.
        But trust me.
        Relax.
        Help is on the way.
        Stay put on this rock
        So they can find you.

But I'm scared.

> Good. You should be scared.
>
> Means your brain is functioning normally.
>
> You've assessed the situation.

But why am I naked?

I think that's when I passed out again.

MARCH 22

The newspaper reported that a couple of volunteers from
Search and Rescue found me at 10 PM that night.
I was in shock, covered with cuts and bruises but no broken bones.
I had a head wound and lost lots of blood.
Hypothermia, of course, was added to the list.
Two guys named Dave and Ernie
had their pictures in the paper.
Two hunters who knew the wilderness area well.
Nothing was mentioned about me being found naked.
(Maybe I imagined that.)

They wrapped me in a blanket
and hauled me out of the woods—
took them until four in the morning.
I remember waking up in the ambulance asking
Where am I?
How is that for original?
The answer was
                    You're in an ambulance.
Which made me laugh
and that hurt like hell
so one guy punched a needle in my arm
and, after a bit,
I settled down
to a dull foggy place inside my head.

I woke up the next day in the middle of the afternoon
and my mom was hovering over me.

Hunter. Thank God.

And my dad came over from the window.

What the hell were you thinking?

And, well, after a couple of dull days
in the hospital
I was back
home.

But sitting in my room
staring at the empty screen of my computer
I felt I was missing something.
Something was not quite right.
There was something I should be remembering.

N.D.E.

I missed school for a week.
I hurt, ached all over
looked like shit in the mirror—
black and blue in the face,
one puffy eye, fat lip.
Every time I moved
it hurt.

But it was my thoughts
that were most upsetting.
                        Fragments:
            lots and lots
of fragments.   Bowling
        (What the hell?)
rain   airplanes
        green grass
            some funny guy talking
always talking   to me.
                        High school
cafeteria
            and a girl
        some girl.

I did some research into   near death
experiences.   N.D.E.

There seems to have been
a lot of tunnels
with light at the end.
But not for me.
(I wondered if I had come close to dying
not really death
but some kind of
mental journey.)

                              No one was reporting
bowling or high school cafeterias or anything like this.
And no one started out leaving this world with clothes on
and returned   naked.
No one.

MOM AND DAD AND A QUICK REVIEW OF ME

Well, they were glad I was alive.
My mother spoiled me by cooking
my favorite things:
>lasagna
>meatloaf
>fried chicken.
This was the upside of nearly dying.
And my dad got over my brazen stupidity
>and asked if I wanted
>a new bike.
I said yes.
>And he said, safety gear.
>You need safety gear.
And hugged me until it hurt.

That night I relived
>my frozen moment of flight
>right before I smashed
>and it went black.
And right then, waking from my sleep
I started to see that face again.
I started to see sunlight and green grass.
>(But no tunnel. Sorry, no tunnel at all.)

I lay there in my bed
that my whole life
marking time
getting by
what would happen

and realized
I'd just been
shuffling my feet
letting the world decide
next.

Finally, on the bike
something had snapped.
           I went balls to the wall.
           (Well, literally, just that.)
And for that frozen airborne glorious moment—
           no—that glorious second
I was   who
I was   meant   to be.

TRIVIAL PURSUIT

The end of March
body healing
no excuses
the end of leftover lasagna
busy parents back to normal lives
and me   back to school.

But that   too   didn't feel right.
I didn't feel like one of them.
            I felt like I'd just arrived
from another planet.
            I got used to kids
pointing at me
laughing at me
asking me about   my story.
What the hell happened out there?
someone asked.
I dunno, man.
I just kind of
fell off my bike.
            (And went somewhere.)
            (Met a girl and went
                  bowling.)
                  (But how could that
                  be?)
No, I didn't say any of that out loud.

I started to study the other kids.
They   seemed to be stuck in something
           seemed to be doing trivial things
           talked about trivial shit
           didn't give a rat's ass
           about important stuff.
                    (Oh, yeah, big shot.)
                    (What's so important?)
This was me and my inner voice again
asking questions I couldn't answer.

And then one day
first day of April
April Fool's Day
surrounded by fools
                    (No, idiot, maybe you're the fool.)
It slammed into me like another wall of granite:
I   did not belong
                       here.

APRIL MADNESS

I kept waiting for clues
                 waiting for pieces of the puzzle
to fit together.

                          And then
I saw   her.
She was alone at her locker.   I
couldn't remember her name.   We'd been friends
once   a long time ago.

Hey, I said.   (Good lad. That took courage.)
         Hi.

                          (Now what? Why am I doing this?)
I stood there like a dope. Nothing to say.
She looked   oh, so unhappy.
You okay? I asked.
         Why?
I dunno. I just looked at you and I thought ...
         Thought what?
Maybe I could   help.   (Help!)
         Hunter.
Yeah.
         Hunter, you haven't even spoken to me
         since, like, sixth grade.
I'm shy.
         No, you're not.

Not now but ...

     What do you want?

Trinity.

     Whoa, nobody's called me that
     for a long time.

But it's your name.

     Yeah,

     but I stopped using it a long time ago.

Why?

     It was my first name.

     I didn't like it. Too weird.

Who are you now?

     I've been Natalie for quite a while.

     It's my middle name.

Can I call you Trinity?

     Why?

I don't know.

     Okay. I guess.

     We used to be friends, right?

Sort of.

     Listen.

     You probably don't want to be friends
     with me now.

Why?

     I'm kind of messed up.

Maybe I can help.   (Way to go, Boy Scout.)

     I wish.

People can be cruel.

     Tell me about it.

Trinity?

      Yeah.

Do you remember sitting with me in an empty cafeteria once?

      When?

I don't know. Not that long ago.

      No. Never.

Shoot.

Do you remember anything about
bowling?

      Hunter,

      you're creeping me out.

      I gotta go.

But we can talk again, right?

      I don't know.

      Maybe.

MORE WEIRD SHIT

Not long after that
     I started to realize
that some kids at school   looked
        different.
It was a gut reaction at first.
     A girl named Lexxie
     had a kind of   glow
     a golden glow

       an aura.
I thought she had died when she was twelve.
     Some kind of rare heart problem.
But here she was and she seemed okay.
The new me stopped her in the hall.
Hey, Lexxie.
     Hunter, hi.
How you feeling?
     Huh?
How is   your health?
     I'm okay. Why?   (Ask her about the aura?)
I don't know. You just have
this kind of glow.   (Nice, dude.)
       (You made her smile.)
     Thanks.   (You silly flirt.)
You're welcome.   (Work it, big boy.)

WALK IT OFF

After school each day, I walked
and walked and walked.
Everywhere I went
seemed more crowded
than it used to be.
The old town was growing, I guess.
More traffic jams
longer lines at the coffee shop.
Could just have been my imagination.

My dad had bought me that new bike.
Not as good as my wrecked one
but he also bought me
helmet, gloves, knee pads, elbow pads.
He was a good
father.

On a sunny day in April, I took
to the woods
stuck to the trails
and it felt
good to be alive.

RIGHT WHERE I LEFT OFF

Wind in my face,
hands gripping the bike
standing on the pedals
blasting on the straight path
                and now everything
was green   very green
      just like
               um ... what was it?
Something   somewhere
but not here.

My last time here was
               back in March
here in the woods
still chilly   barren trees
oh, and that intimate encounter
with an immovable object.
             That was about as real
as a thing can get
             but now I had this feeling
that when I woke up   way back then
      it wasn't in an ambulance.

I stopped
threw down the helmet
and sat down
on a patch of
grass.

Holy shit
I said out loud.

got off my bike
    took a deep breath

Then it hit me
harder
than
granite.

PROFESSIONAL HELP

I rode home   (helmet on, hands gripping.
                                Mr. Safety now.)
Guess I didn't want to die   again.

Kitchen scene   (always a great location
                                to tell your folks about
                                what happened after
                                you died).
Mom   Dad
it went like this.

                    Well, you know the tale
                            the tale so far.

They sat and stared at first.
            (is this really our son?)
            (Could be a brain injury.)
            (Could be drugs.)
            Do you really believe this happened?
                    my dad asked.
Yes.
It happened.
            My mom said, Hunter, we love you, but ...
            But, my dad interrupted, Yeah, son, we love you but
            you need professional help.
So they took me to my doctor and then   to a shrink.

WHAT THE SHRINK SAID

Doctor Felson   was his name.
I told my story.   It was vivid now
                the whole package
                so clear
                kind of like
a Disney movie with a really weird script
like the producer had turned his back
and the scriptwriter and director had conspired
to really mess with the audience
until they didn't know what the hell the flick
                    was about.

Felson was bald with a really shiny head
that reminded me of
        a bowling ball.
He had nice eyes and seemed   kind
and didn't act like he was listening
               to an insane young man.

        Okay, he said, finally.
        I've heard stories like this before.
        Well, not exactly like this.
        Yours is rather   what shall we say
        creative   but
        let's work with it.

WORKING WITH IT

Who seemed to be in charge, he asked
at this place you went to?
I'm not sure but there was this guy.
        Ah, your advisor.
Yes. How did you know?
        Just guessing.   Others
        have mentioned meeting someone   a guide.
Well, he seemed to be just that.
Archie.
He said his name was Archie.
        A dead relative?
        Grandfather perhaps?
My grandfathers are named
Mike
and Peter   and they're
                                       both alive.

        Hmm.
        You didn't know him?
Never met him before
in my life.   (Saying that last part
                                       made me feel really funny.)

Doc made a kind of tent with his fingers
and stared at his manicured nails
thinking, I guess, about
what to say next.

Well
I've seen the scans   of your brain
and I didn't see anything of significance
but then
a trauma   is a trauma.
                (The man was brilliant, you could tell.)
And I don't like to prescribe   drugs
for every little bit of anxiety   or worry.
                (Great news, Doc, but I don't think
                this is about feeling antsy over
                a math test.
                We're talking death here
                and a free trip back.)
So
let's think of it   this way.

THE WAY I SHOULD VIEW THE WHOLE SHEBANG

I think, he said   you should
live with the experience
and don't necessarily believe   it to be true
but don't
deny it, either.
Work with it.   It's your … um …
narrative.
He explained that
his version of treatment was something called
narrative therapy.
I was the protagonist
in my   story.
(And, oh, what an off-the-rails Hollywood story it was.)
          Come back in a week.
Should I tell others about what happened to me?
          I don't know, should you?
They'll think I'm crazy.
          Some will. Some won't.
But now   everything
seems so   … well …
unimportant.   How do I
cope?
(And then it got a little weirder.)
          Just go
          with the flow, he said.
(And he smiled.)

PIECES OF THE PUZZLE

I sat down with a piece of paper
and made a list:
green grass, Archie, clouds, crowd,
rain, Trinity, bowling, coffee …
that didn't get me anywhere.

Archie seemed to be at the center of things.
And no, he did not come
from anywhere in my life.
Why Archie?
Archie, short for Archibald.
      (Let's look it up.)
Means "bold and true"
or "genuine, brave, and bold."
      (Well, that helps.)
Most popular as a name in the 1890s but went downhill after
that.
Nicknames: Arch, Arc, Itch, Archeese, Cheese.
    (Now, we're getting somewhere.
    Nice to think that my one-time guru
    had something to do with
    coagulated milk protein.)
No, must be more.
Archie short for archangel?   (Do I really want to go there?)

"A high-ranking angel."

(Just doesn't seem to fit my guy.)

Worth a Wikichase anyway:
Gabriel, Michael, Azrael, Israfel.

(Checked their creds.
No way did they fit Archie
of the Green Grass.)

BUT THEN THERE WAS THIS

Funny thing about fooling around on the Internet
—after you've died and come back to Google—
is that you just might stumble   (even a random stumble)
onto some mighty interesting shit.

Like this.
Archangel led me to plain "arch" which led me straight to
                              archetype
and someone named Carl Jung (which I thought was the name
of
a non-alcoholic wine that I had seen in the supermarket).
Mr. Jung studied myths and religions
                around the planet
                              and determined
                there were   twelve
human archetypes.   I'd never heard
the word before   .   but
it refers to "universal types or patterns."
Double holy shit.
                      For your edification
(if you are not a Jungian)   they are:
The Innocent, The Everyman, The Hero,
The Caregiver, The Explorer, The Rebel,
The Lover, The Creator, The Jester,
The Sage, The Magician, The Ruler.

Now, I know what you're thinking.
You do not solve life / death mysteries   with
Wikipedia
but my brain was   on fire.
See

                    we all
have qualities of
each of these archetypes   but
one of these types   dominates who we are.
(My dad, unlike Jung, once told me after drinking seven beers
that there are only two types of people in the world:
        assholes
        and people who have to put up with assholes
        but it could have been the Bud speaking.)
But let's get serious, class.

                    Let's say that each of us
is primarily six of the twelve A-types.

                    Why am I saying this?
Because I knew right then that I was
The Innocent (Never knew squat back in the day.) /
The Everyman (Plain ole me.) /
The Hero (Hey, it's my story!) /
The Explorer (Why else fly into a granite wall?) /
The Lover (Hell, yes.) /
The Caregiver (Hmm.)   Okay, okay. Maybe not the
old me.

                    But the new me wanted to look out
                    for Trinity. (Whose name means
three

                    which is half of six.)

And I'm gambling here, but I think this new me
　　　this new Caregiver
just trumped　　　　　　　the other five.

Okay, okay, settle down, class.
　　　　　　Yes, I probably have lost my
　　　mind
but　　　　　　　　　　　　if
I really did die
　　　and have come　　　　　back
and I am trying to figure some serious shit out.

You better　　　　　　　　　　　　listen up.

THEORY—THIS IS ONLY A THEORY.

So, now if I am the Innocent / Everyman / Explorer aspiring to be the
Caregiving / Loverboy / Hero
well, that makes me half of the full canon of what makes up us humans.

        Am I not correct?

And, therefore, I need
to see my other half
when I leave this little blue planet
for the infinite lawn of eternity   (or whatever)
so that's why I run into   Archie:
The Rebel / Creator / Jester / Sage / Magician / Ruler.

Archie, are you listening?
Cause I don't have your number yet   but
I can see there's a lot of   power in that package
and I want to know
which of those archetypes
is really
in charge.

MEET DAVIS COOPER

And then   a little further along
on this new revised earthly timeline
                         that didn't seem quite real
I ran into   this kid
                         named Davis Cooper.

     Yo, he said.
     You one of us?
It was outside school   and raining   cold rain.
Late April rain.   This kid with long wet hair   and a
shit-eating grin.   Thirteen years old, maybe.
I just looked at him   this ballsy kid
who didn't know how to get in out of the rain.
     Hunter, right?
     Hunter Callaghan?
Who are you?
     Davis   Davis Cooper   and I saw
     that you had that look.
What look?
     C'mon, you know.   (Goofy kid smiling again.)
You think I'm gay?
     No. Not that. But I don't care if you are. Doesn't matter.
I'm not gay.
     Glad we got that out of the way.
     So, tell me. How was it?

It?

On the other side?

So there. He slammed me into another rock face.

Caught me off guard.

What is it you see? I asked.

You give off light.

You can see this?

Yes.

And, oh shit, now I see him. Really see him.

So do you, I said.

I know.

LESLEY CHOYCE

RANDOM

How did it happen? I asked.
How did you end up   there?
        I was minding my own business.
        Walking down Main Street.
        Just after dark.
And?
        Car came by with someone hanging out the window
        who happened to have   a gun.
        Don't know who he was aiming for
        but maybe he didn't care.
        Maybe I was just a random
        victim.
        Funny, huh?
You died?
        Died and came back.
        Crazy, huh?
        But then   you
        you came back, too.
What happened when …?
        When I was dead?
Yes, when you were dead.
        Met this guy there
        on the other side.
Archie?
        How'd you know?

I just know.

    Oh.

What did he tell you?

    Maybe it was all a dream.

What did he say?

    I had only been there
    for a short time.
    I kind of   liked the place.

What did he say?

    He said I had to go back
    here.

Why?

    It didn't make any sense
    but then   I was
    pretty disoriented.

But he sent you back and it was like it never happened?
The shooting?

    Yeah, I was just back on Main Street
    minding my own business.

Of course you were.

But what did Archie say?

    Something really weird.
    Something about   closing down
    heaven.

DEAD OR NOT DEAD

So you died and came back.
   I don't know, man.
   It was more like a dream
   but not a dream   if
   that makes any sense.
But you see an aura around some people?
   A glow.
   You have it.
I think I've seen it, too. On others, I mean.
   What about me?
   How do I look?
      I had to squint
   but there was definitely something there.
Yeah, I can see it clearly now. Kind of bright.
Coppery.
Didn't notice it at first.
Who else?
   Well, some people on the street.
   Old folks, some kids.
   You know a girl named Lexxie?
Yeah. I thought she died when she was like, twelve.
   She probably did.
Davis, how do you make sense of all this?
   Hey, I'm just a kid.
   A lot of shit doesn't make sense
   to me.

I just go with the flow.
Where'd you get that line from?

Davis gave me a funny look.
I know where you heard that.

Yeah, Archie told me a lot of stuff.
Some true stuff. Maybe some stuff
not so true.

COMMUNION

Davis, I got somebody I want you to meet.
       I gotta get to class.
It's important.
       So is the test in English.
What about noon?
In the cafeteria?
       Can do.
See you then.

I found Trinity / Natalie after much difficulty.
       Hunter, what's wrong?
Nothing. I want you to meet
someone.
       What's this about?
It's about you and me
and where we met.
       Hunter, you're crazy.
Follow me.

We found Davis by the door of the caf.
He was just standing there   playing
a video game on his phone.
       Shit, he said. I lost again
Davis, this is Trinity. I mean Natalie.
       (Trinity looked like she was about to run.)
It's okay, Natalie. Just trust me.

Davis, what do you see?

      I see light. Blue light.

            Who is this? Trinity asked.

Davis Cooper. He sees auras.

      Only on some people.

      It's usually yellow or gold

      —or even white—

      but never blue.

            Is this some kind of stupid joke?

No.   (I squinted again.)

I can see it, too.

      I gotta go, Davis said.

      You guys sort this out.

            I'm not sorting out anything, she said.

And she turned to go.

GAMES

Wait, Natalie. Don't go.
>Hunter, I got enough problems.
>I don't want anything to do with
>your weird games.

It's not a game.
There's something special
about you
and something I shared with
you.
>(Her look said she was scared.
>I was scaring her.)

Will you go someplace with me
after school?
>Where?

I want to take you bowling.

THE WORST BOWLERS ON THE PLANET

Yes, we were bad.
I don't think
in a long

But I made her laugh.
the girl had laughed
long time.

LESLEY CHOYCE

AFTERWARD

She said she had fun
as I walked her home   this sad girl
who I had made laugh.
      I like you, she said.
      I always did.
Cool, I said.   (Like an idiot.)
      But the problem is
      I'm already seeing someone.
Oh. Who?
      Jake.
No, not Jake.
      Yes. Jake.
(My memory about the other place was much, much clearer now.)
(She had told me about Jake.)
(Jake the jerk)
(Jake the asshole)
I just don't think he's right.
      What does that mean?
Not right for you.
Not good for you.
      You don't know him.
You told me he treated you like shit.
      I never told you that.
(Damn. She told me this on the other side.)
(She doesn't remember.)
(Why do I remember?)

(Don't push this. Back off.)

Sorry. I was confused.

       Yeah, very confused.

       Jake has his problems but

       I think I'm in love with him.

       He's not like

       the others.

Trinity.

Natalie.

I just want you to be okay.

       I *am* okay.

TIMELINE

Okay.   If I knew what was going on
              if I knew what the truth was
              if I knew where I had really gone
              if I knew why I was back here
maybe things would make more sense
and maybe I could do the right thing
              but
I   was   missing   pieces
of the puzzle.

Timeline:
I died March 21.
Davis died April 17.
It was now April 29.
Trinity said she took the pills on
                              June 15
        one week before school was out.
                    This means
                    Trinity
                    in this timeline
                    didn't die
                    yet.
But does it still mean
                    she *will*
                    die?

DISTANCE

Trinity kept her distance from me   after that.
I tried to talk to her   but she always just said
       Hunter. Don't.
I kept thinking she'd remember   but she didn't.
Maybe because   well
for her   it hadn't happened
yet.
I saw her with   Jake.
                 Jake the jerk
                 Jake, the cool but mean guy
                 Jake, who knew how to get a girl interested
                 use her
                 and then treat her like shit.
But Trinity wouldn't listen. Natalie wouldn't listen.

ROLLING INTO MAY

In my dreams   I was back there.
I was looking for Archie.
But he wasn't around.   What if
I had imagined   the whole thing?

If I squinted, I could see other people on the street
with auras.   All adults.
I tried
to stop and talk to a couple of them
but they thought I was trying to hustle them for money
or they thought I was on drugs.
If they too had died
and come back
they couldn't remember
or were denying it .
or maybe
I was just
insane.

I guess I was looking for   some kind of
confirmation
but I wasn't getting anywhere
so   I rode my bike
into the woods and   sat on a boulder
at Lost Lake
thinking.   Just thinking.

Archie, I said out loud
looking up at the clouds.
Archie, come tell me what to do!
But all there was
was
wind   and sky   and silence.

DAVIS

By the end of May   I stopped trying
to make sense of anything.   I stopped trying
to talk to Trinity.   I stopped trying
to find that pipsqueak Davis
        who couldn't be found in school
        and his friends didn't know where he was
        and I thought maybe he went back.
(Can you do that? Can you get called back?)
(If so, take me now. Let me back in!)

And then one day
           there he was
           the nerdy little guy.
Davis, I said
where the hell were you?
        Europe, he said.
        My parents took me to Europe.
        How are things, Hunter?
I'm having a hard time.
        With what?
Everything.
        Sucks to be you.
Can you help?
        How?
Start with Archie. Tell me what you know about Archie.
        You know, I thought he was the real deal.

But now I don't know.

I think he was a bullshitter.

What do you mean?

I think he was a kind of trickster.

In Europe, I was doing some reading.

In every culture, there's a trickster.

You think Archie lied to us?

I think he may be a kind of joker or clown.

(This was starting to remind me of Carl Jung.)

(How could this kid know about that?)

You think he had us sent back as some kind of joke?

I try not to think about it too much.

It hurts my head.

Maybe it's all a joke.

When I came back, I was naked.

That's not the way I left.

Bad joke, I'd say.

But there are others. I see their auras.

Me too, but no one seems to remember.

Maybe they've been tricked, too.

But why?

Who knows? Hard to figure out
the big picture
so I stopped trying.
Time to get on
with my so-called life.

Davis, you ever try to communicate
with Archie?

Yes.

How?

     Self-hypnosis.

Can you teach me?

     Probably.

     But here's the thing.

     I don't think Archie

     will give you anything straight.

     In fact, I think

     that whole story about

     closing down heaven

     wasn't true

     at all.

SELF-HYPNOSIS

Davis explained it to me
and gave me a book.

                                    All you had to do was
lie down
relax every part of your body
    (Your toes are feeling very relaxed.)
step by step.   (Relax your foot
                relax your ankles
                relax your calves
and knees and thighs and hips and lower back and upper back
and
chest and shoulders and neck and chin and mouth and nose
and
eyes
and back of your head and top of your head
and count backwards
10 9 8 7 6 5 4 3 2 1
and then remain
very very very relaxed.)

WHEN AT FIRST

It took me three tries   but on the third try
I knew
I was very deep.   I was
self-hypnotized.   And I liked it a lot.
You should try it.   It works.

Archie, I silently asked. I need to speak with you.
Yo, Arch.

                    Silence and light
                    (The light surprised me.)
Archie?

                    More silence and light
This time, though, more silent than before and even brighter
and then

            Hunter?
            How did you get here?
Davis Cooper told me how.

            The kid's a menace.
            Precocious little dweeb.
I could see a fuzzy image of someone.
Archie.

            Don't try to focus, Hunter.
            That would be bad.
            You're not supposed to be here.
Why not?

            Because you're alive, nitwit.

We try to keep a clean line
between this side and your side.

Why?

Because that's the way it works.
In fact, I'm not sure
we should be having this conversation.

I've seen others   the glow   the inner light.

Every living thing has an aura.
Electromagnetic energy, Sherlock.
It's no big deal.
Look, I gotta go.
This is against code.

But there's something you need to tell me.

I know, I know.
But not
yet.

When then?

When you finish up
with what you have to do.

JAKE JONES

What mother would name her kid Jake Jones?
Jake was on the soccer team—star halfback.
Jake was tall, well built, smooth talker, move maker
manipulator   and a guy
who always got what he wanted.
Always.
Especially   when it came to
girls.   There had been many.
I could remember seven in recent memory
all nice girls   smart girls   vulnerable girls
that he swept away to the Planet of the Jakes.

Jake had hardly ever talked to me.
         I wasn't on his radar anymore because
         I had nothing he wanted.
But let me take you back to when
I was ten years old.
I was as good at soccer as Jake was back then
and
we played on the school team.
We liked each other.
We worked together   passing the ball
back and forth   running down the field
and when we neared the goal,   it was Jake   always Jake
who scored. Always.   But then one day
I changed the rules.   At the last second

I didn't   pass the ball to Jake.
I kicked hard.   I scored.
Jake never passed the ball to me again.
And once, we collided.   No, he smashed into me
and kicked me hard   in the crotch
and smiled.

These days, Jake was scoring in other ways.

I'm trying to be fair here, though.
I'm sure he had his good side
but his great skill was   telling a girl
what she wanted to hear.   And that
along with the fame (of sorts)
the golden boy looks
and the fact   that every girl in school
wanted to be seen   with him
made scoring easy.

THE MERRY MONTH OF MAY

Near the end of the month
I began to understand what Davis had been feeling.
My longing to go back to that place
was fading.

The Explorer / Hero / Lover / Caregiver
was fading and all that was left was
the Innocent / Everyman.
But I kept thinking about Trinity—
our brief time in that other place   our cosmic bowling
and all the rest.
The time I spent with her.
That did not go away.
The word "destiny"   (I know, I know)
haunted me.
The online dictionary calls it

        "An inevitable,
irresistible   pre-determined
course of events."

        No.

No.   No.   No.
It can't be like that.

Deep in my self-induced trance   (I was getting better
going deeper)   I walked up on Archie
from behind.   Only it
wasn't Archie.   When he turned around
it was Jake.   A version of Jake
much older   with a hideous face
laughing
at me.

WHEN I WOKE UP

Yes, woke up.
That was just   a dream
I told myself   but   I started to reflect
on what Davis had said.   Maybe Archie
was a trickster.   Aha.   Perhaps
he embodied   (stay with me)   the other six
archetypes:
Rebel (who didn't play by the rules)
Sage (too smart for his own good)
Jester (a trickster getting a good laugh out of my predicament)
Magician (indeed, hocus-pocus, smoke and mirrors of the mind)
Ruler (his game, his rules)   or worse yet
Creator (and there is the scariest one of all).

JUNE 6

History Class.
D-Day   June 6, 1944.
Allied troops land on the beaches of Normandy in WWII.
On this day, in 1944, Mr. Blomquist (Mr. Consequences) said
there was death and destruction
and the beginning of the end
of the war.
But it was hell for many.

After listening about the war
I realized
it was
a good day to go to the woods   after school.
Deep into the woods   past Lost Lake
past all the other lakes   and on deeper into the woods.
Pedaling my ass off   pumping hard
past the end
of the trail.   Wind   in my face
and bugs   and off-trail challenges
thorns   and rocks   and tangled vines.

Got lost at first   or thought so
but then it all looked   so familiar
and suddenly   I was
where I needed to be:

the place I crashed
the place I died
the place I came back
naked.
(If a godlike trickster was going to send you back from being dead,
would he not want to have a good laugh
by sending a teenage boy
back to the woods
naked?)

Okay, Dr. Felson, what is the narrative here?
Boy sits back down in the woods and stares
at his boulder of destiny
waits for the rock to apologize.
Decides it could take millennia.
Instead, he realizes
he must figure out a way
to speak again with Archie
and decide
on a course   of action.

What now?
        Lie down.
        Full relaxation.
        Go deep.
     Hunter, the voice says.
     You don't need to do that.
It's Archie.   I open my eyes.
     Fancy meeting you here, he says.

Yeah, fancy that.

> You don't seem to be fully settled
> back into your old life.

I know. Sucks to be me.

> But you're one of the lucky ones, lad.

Lucky?

> You get to pick up where you left off
> and you remember everything
> about being dead.

Maybe that's what makes it so hard.

> Why?

I

… well …

liked it there.

Didn't want to leave.

> My mistake.

You make mistakes?

> We all make mistakes.

How do I know for sure I can trust you?

> You don't.

Then why are you here?

> You wanted to see me.

> And I was tired of getting
> … well … all your doubts.

What?

> Every time you questioned something
> it was like an annoying phone call
> or text message or email
> that I didn't want to deal with.

So?

So I'm here.

Ask away.

Davis Cooper says you can't be trusted.

He's a nerdy kid whose parents take him to Europe.

He doesn't know diddly.

But he died and came back
like me.

I told you, you weren't alone.

He said that they're not really
closing down heaven
not sending everyone back.

That's partly true.

Then you lied to me.

We don't call it lying.

There are various timelines.

In one timeline   heaven is shutting down.

And in other timelines?

We just send some people back.

Like me?

Like you.

And Davis?

Yes. He was too annoying to keep.

And Lexxie.

She was sweet
but had major unfinished business.

And Trinity.

What about
her?

Silence.

More silence.

Well?

You met her on the other side
for a reason.

What reason is that?

I don't know.

What about June 15?

What about it?

June 15.

She overdoses.

She dies.

It hasn't happened yet.

Not in this timeline.

(Suddenly I felt very, very tired.)

END OF THE CONVERSATION

Tell me what to do.
        I can't.
Guide me.
I thought you were
my mentor.
        Not down here.
        This was just a courtesy call.
        I don't really have much
        influence here.
Then leave me alone.
        I will.
        But, Hunter
        be careful.
        You're a tiny player
        in a big game.
        A game too big
        for anyone
        including me
        to figure it all out.
Just one more thing.
        Shoot.
Is Archie your real name?
        Yes.
        Archie's my real name.

FORGET ABOUT CAREFUL

As I rode my bike   out of the woods
I was feeling like   I'd been jerked around.
Freaking Archie
     was messing with me
     teasing me
     giving me half-clues
     giving me mixed messages
     playing games with me
like I was a little nobody player in a complex game
     and only he   knew the rules.
I was   a gladiator in an arena
     I hadn't built
     and didn't know what I was fighting
     and didn't know what weapons to use
     but I damn well knew
     there was an audience.
     An audience of one, at least.

Time to assert   free will.
Meet destiny
     or punch destiny in the face.
         (Hunter, is this the new you?)
Time is running out.

(In this timeline
as Archie would say
but then, screw Archie.)
Maybe there is only one timeline.
One life.
One chance to make things right.

JAKE JONES

Natalie / Trinity was avoiding me.
Saw her down the hall
and she was hugging her books
and looked hurt
really hurt.
But
she ran
        whenever I was in sight.
            The other piece of this puzzle was
Jake.
      So   I started stalking him.
Locker—   messy.
Lunch—   pizza and a doughnut.
Soccer field— still hogging the glory.
Street—   the guy littered, for God's sake.
Home—   fancy house, tidy yard.
And then this: a girl
Chloe   (Chloe of the Clothes
              or should I say Clones?
              She was so like the other girls
              in her crowd.)
Chloe arrived at Jake's house   and rang the doorbell.
And Jake
(yes, Jake)   answered
and kissed her hard
kicked the door shut

and then   then
I could see them
through the open window
of what must have been   Jake's
bedroom ...
          Jake, you scummy manslut.

MAN ON A MISSION

I knew
what I had to do.
        I had to tell Trinity
            what I saw.
Trouble was this: I was out
of my depth.   Hunter Callaghan
knew next to nothing   about girls
and how to   properly communicate
with them.

Question:
How do you get to be sixteen and never have a real girlfriend?
Answer:
Just watch Hunter Callaghan as he grows up.

Nonetheless   something had
to be done.   So
I went to her house.
I used to walk there sometimes
back in the sixth grade
but never had the nerve
to walk up and ring the bell.
As I walked, I wondered
if this was the right thing
to do.
I decided
it was.

Trinity, I said, you have to listen to me.

> I'd rather you don't call me that.

Natalie, I really care about you.

> What?

I like you.

> You came here to tell me this?

I don't want to see you get hurt but …

> (I'm creeping her out again, I know.)

> But what?

It's Jake.

> What about Jake?

He's with Chloe.

> What do you mean, *with* Chloe?

Now. I just saw him.

> Where?

At his house.

> You were spying on Jake?

Yes.

> And you've been stalking me, too, right?

Not stalking.

> Then what?

Trying to …

> Trying to do what?

Keep you from getting hurt.

> You already said that.

Jake is not the guy for you.

> Was he really with Chloe?

Yes.

> Why are you telling me this?

Because I know what will happen.

No.

I mean, what *can* happen.

And what can happen, Hunter?

I can't tell you.

In her face I see:

pain

confusion

fear

rage.

Door Slams in Boy's Face on Darkest Day of the Year.

BLUE AURA

She had it.   I could see it clearly.
     The blue aura.
It hovered in the air for a few seconds
     even after the door was closed.
And I wished Davis Cooper   had never
drawn my attention to seeing auras.
I thought about banging on the door   but
everything had gone badly.
What if?
What if?
     What if my news
     sends her over the edge?
What if it's today   and not
   June 15?

NARRATIVE THERAPY

Well, I didn't know where to turn.
So
I went to see Dr. Felson.

> You really think she'll try to hurt herself? he asked
> matter-of-factly.

Yes.

> Could be you're projecting.

What does that mean?

> Maybe *you* are thinking of suicide.

Bullshit.

> Just checking.

It's not me.

> But didn't you already
> try to do it
> when you slammed your bike
> into that boulder?

No way.
That was the opposite.
That was me
trying to really live.

> Sorry.
> You're sure you're okay?

Yes.
Well …
no.

> You're ambivalent.

What does that mean?

    You're okay but

    you're not okay.

    Why?

I saw the blue aura again.

    Around her?

Even after she was gone. I saw it.

    What do you think it means?

I don't know.

    Maybe you should find out.

How?

    (Felson put his hands in the air

    and gave a most professional shrug.)

Great.

    Hunter, are you going to be okay?

I don't know.

IN SEARCH OF THE BLUES

I walked to the most crowded
part of town
and squinted   at person after person.
I saw   some yellow
        some orange
        even some fuzzy kind of gray-white light
        but no blues.
So I went to the place
I did   not want   to go.
        The hospital.
I hung around the emergency entrance
but it was a quiet day.   No action.
So
I
went
inside.

Bad memories crept in
of waking up here
in pain.
It made me antsy
and afraid
but I ran up two flights of stairs
and my heart started beating
fast.
I opened the door on the third floor

LESLEY CHOYCE

and it was so quiet.
I ignored the staring nurse sitting at a desk
and went down the hall.
I peeked in every door
that was open
and saw   old people
                sick people
                people in pain
but then I saw

                      one old woman
                      lying on her back
                      eyes closed
                      mouth open
                      oxygen tubes up her nose
                      monitor by the bed
                      and one hell of a display
                      of light
                      emanating from her.

I wanted to run   but didn't.
Instead, I walked up to her
and took her hand
and leaned close
and whispered, it's going to be okay.
You don't have anything to worry about.
You're going to   love it   there.

And I thought I saw a hint of a smile
or it could have been my   imagination.
And I don't know why

but I kissed her
on the cheek
and left.

I left the room then
and began to walk back down the hall
but
it didn't quite
sink in
until
some kind of alarm went off
and some nurses
started running
to her room.

OUTSIDE THE HOSPITAL

I sat down on the curb
and cried.
I felt sad about the old lady
and wondered
if my few words
had triggered something.
        After all
        I had told her
        it was okay
        to die.
What did that make me?
So I cried some more
and then started walking
feeling more confused
than I'd ever felt.
More than anything
I wished
that I didn't know
what I
knew.
And I felt   totally   helpless
and lost.

DARKNESS

I just kept walking
until the sun had gone down
                and it was dark.
But I just kept walking
and by then I was downtown
on a busy street   when I heard a voice
                        a soft woman's voice
                        the voice of a very old lady

        say
    Go back to her, Hunter.
    She's in trouble.

ALL ALONE IN THE WORLD

That's how I felt
as I ran.
I felt the weight
of what I knew
and what I   somehow
had to do.

So I ran
all the way back to Trinity's house
        only to hear

                  a siren

    and see

                  an ambulance

racing away.

THE END OF THE ROAD

They wouldn't let me see her
at the hospital.   Her parents
screamed at me
                         when they figured out
I was the one
who had told her about Jake.
A security guard   grabbed me
and dragged me out of the building.

Two days later
I learned
that Trinity
was gone.

WHAT A BOY FEELS

Despair is a word that comes close.
Hopeless despair
and guilt.
I had thought I was doing
                  the right thing
by telling her   about Jake the Snake.

But
I had done   the absolute
                wrong thing.
And now   she was gone.
Already
I missed her.
Yes.
I thought   I could have saved her.
I thought   I had until June 15.
But she died
on June 10.
How could that be?
But then
I didn't understand
any of this.

And more than ever
more than before   I felt
that I didn't

belong
here.

Not now.
Not anymore.

DARK PLACES

I went to some
very dark places   and discovered
I could not live   with myself
not here   not now.
The dark swallowed me
and I lived inside it
if you could call this living.

My parents were worried
and tried to help   but
I was very far away
in my wilderness of despair.

I tried to contact Archie
for news
but he was not there.
I tried to contact Trinity
to say I was sorry
but she was silent.   Everything was silent.

But then I woke up   on June 15
and it was a bright warm day
and the birds were singing
in the trees with green leaves
and the sun was bright
and I watched a plane

flying high overhead
                    and I knew it was time
                    to get back on my bike.

My dad insisted
that I put on the helmet
and pads   but I knew
                        I wasn't going   to need them.
And besides
I wasn't going   into the woods.
I wasn't going   far at all.

I had just got my bike out of the garage
and was rolling down the driveway when
                    I see this kid
                    nerdy little Davis Cooper
                    walking toward me.
            There you are, he said.
            Where have you been?
            You haven't been in school.
Leave me alone, I said.
            Hunter, I'm sorry about Trinity.
Fuck off.
            I thought maybe you could save her.
            I feel really bad about what happened.
This isn't about you.
            I should have stayed out of it.
            I should have kept my mouth shut
            about the auras.
Yes, you should have.

Now fuck off.

      Hunter, don't do it.

(There was no way he could know.)

I'm not doing anything.

I just want you to leave me alone.

And I got on my bike   pedaled

as hard   and as fast

as I could.   Inside my head

I was

screaming.

SO THIS IS HOW IT WENT

I felt like I was doing the right thing.
                              the only thing
I could do.

I felt no fear
I had no doubt   no second thoughts   no ambivalence.
It seemed perfectly reasonable.
So I did it.

I rode to the stop light
by the highway.
It was red.
The cars and trucks were speeding by.
I saw the one.
A big truck
moving fast.
I kicked down hard
on the pedals.
My timing was   perfect.

LESLEY CHOYCE

I KNOW WHAT YOU'RE THINKING

My decision hurt a lot of people.
Yes.
It did.
But I could not live with the pain and guilt.
I am sorry.
I know I hurt my parents deeply.
I felt bad for the driver of the truck
and
the people who watched.
I felt bad for the man
who tried to breathe air into my lungs
and make my heart work again.
But I left the scene
quickly   and ended up
inside a cloud   (fog maybe)
but there was no earth under me.
I guess you could say   I was floating
but the thing I wasn't prepared for
was that I could not tell   what was me
and what was not.   I waited
for a long time   a really long time
for something   anything.
But there was only the fog   the mist   the cloud
that had swallowed me.

TIME

After a while   time did not seem to exist
or matter.
I couldn't remember why I was here
or where *here* was.
I didn't seem to care   much
about anything.   I was lost
but it didn't seem to matter.   I felt
no emotions
had   no expectations
              no sense that anything   not even me
was real.   Or ever was real.
                              And then
for no apparent reason   my old mountain bike
              appeared.
It was good as new.
And the mist began to clear a little
                              and I could see   a path
through a forest.
And I began to realize   I had feet
and legs   and arms   and a body.
Yes, I had a body   just like the good old days.

So I got on the bike and put on the helmet
that was hanging on the handlebars
              and I began to ride
              and it felt great.
And suddenly   I began   to care.

_____

LESLEY CHOYCE

IMAGES

Images of everything flashed by as I rode through the forest.
I saw my parents.
I saw my hometown and school and people and I saw
everything at once.   Everything.
And then   I got dizzy, so
I got off my bike and sat on a rock. (No, not that rock.)
And then
she was there.

       Hi, she said.
Trinity.

       I guess you can call me that now.
I'm sorry.

       Sorry you told me about Jake?
Yes.

       That doesn't seem to be important to me now.
What is important?
Now?

       What's important is you and me.

       Otherwise we wouldn't be doing this.
Doing what?

       Talking.

       Trying to figure things out.
I came here for you.

       I know. That was stupid.
But I'm here.
You're here.

       I guess we're in this together.

Whatever *this* is.

You haven't figured it all out?

Not really.

All I know is that

I came here to be with you.

Why?

Because I felt I had to.

I chose to.

A little free will can kill ya.

And did.

This is all because you remembered me from sixth grade?

Something like that.

THE NEXT BIG THING

What do you think happens next? I asked her.
      I think it all depends on whether
        we still have free will   or not.
Let me try something.
      What?

So I kissed her and she kissed me back   and it seemed
very
very
very
real.

ARCHIE RETURNS

And that's when Archie made his appearance.
        Hello, he said. Just like old times.
I'd given up on you.
        I don't blame you. But I'm here.
Wherever here is.
        You know where you're at.
        And why.
We want to be able to be together, I said, looking at Trinity.
        You are together.
        But you're not supposed to be here.
        Either one of you.
Why?
        Don't you remember?
        They're closing down heaven.
I thought that was all a lie.
        Not in this timeline it isn't.
I never understood about the timeline thing.
        Most people don't.
        I'm not sure I do
        but there are many timelines
        for all of us.
        Which ones are real? Trinity asked.
Yeah, which ones?
        All of them.
Bullshit.
        Sorry, it's not bullshit.

It's just not easy to comprehend.
We just want to stay here, Trinity said.
Like this.

Trouble is …

What?

Trouble is, after a while, you will lose …
Um … your identity—
who you are.
And then you become
part of everything.
No longer Hunter.
No longer Trinity.

So?

So you'll miss out
Miss out on what?
You'll miss out on what you could have had
before things got, well, complicated.

PICKING UP THE PIECES

Do you really mean we can pick up where we left off?

                  More or less.

That's a scary thought.

                  You two have to decide

                  If you want to be

                  together

                  and if

                  you truly want to go

                  back.

I want us to be together.

                  Trinity?

        I think so but

        everything back there

        was so painful.

Then we should stay here.

Together.

                  You'll be back eventually.

                  What's the rush?

        If we do go back

        what will be different?

                  You'll remember some of this.

                  But it will be a different timeline.

                  Enough to make everything different.

How?

                  Leave that to us.

LAST DAY OF SCHOOL

Trinity and I had just finished our final final exam of the year.
We walked out of school into the sunlight.

Something seemed different about this year, she said.
I felt that way, too.

It's because we found each other.
Why did we wait so long?

I don't know. But I'm glad we did.
You still have those dreams?

Yeah. You?
Yeah, but not so much.
Funny, though, that we both had such similar ones.

What do you think that means?
I don't know.
I think it just means we were meant to be together.

Why didn't we figure that out sooner?
Could have saved us both a lot of pain.

That's for sure. What do we do now?
School's out. More time for us.
Let's get the bikes and head into the woods.

Absolutely.
God, it feels good to be alive.

It couldn't be any better.

HAUNTED

Haunted is the word, although it's not quite right.
I'm haunted by   the way my life could have gone
                 the way my life did go
                        in those other timelines
the ones I can remember.
They're fading, however
but I wanted to hold onto the memories
before they're gone.

I don't say some things out loud
to Trinity
or to anyone.
Some days I feel the responsibility
(a word I always hated).
I feel the weight of who I am
what I am:
the guy who is here to take care of Trinity.
Is that why I'm here
or is there more?
                    Archie is not
                    answering my questions
                    anymore.
And then there is this feeling inside me
that I am different from almost
                        everyone else.

It's because of where I've been
what I've lived through

                        (and died through).
I see things differently.
The trivial things

                        people are caught up in.
The games.
The bullshit.
I want to tell everyone

                how it really is.
But I've learned not to do that.
So I keep it to myself.

BRIGHT AND YELLOW

Once I started talking to Trinity about the dreams
                              the memories
or whatever
          she shared hers as well.
Some days it all seems vivid and real
          but now
I'm   so caught up in living
                              really living
this life
that I think
it's maybe all just an illusion.
I can still   see her glow   her aura
but it's bright and yellow   and she says
she can see mine   but maybe this
is just a game we play.   Maybe it's all
just a game.   We'll probably never
ever   understand the rules
but the best thing to do is to play *this* game
like our lives
depend on it.

LESLEY CHOYCE

INTERVIEW WITH LESLEY CHOYCE

Where did this story originate for you?

This was one of those novels where the title suddenly presented itself to me one morning shortly after waking up. I didn't know what it meant or what the story was about, but the title haunted me for a month or so. This is usually a good thing that gets some creative juices flowing.

Although I have no more clues than the next person about what happens after we die, I've always been fascinated by the possibilities. Probably our minds are too limited to fully grasp where we fit into the big scheme of things and what becomes of "us" after we die. The beauty of fiction is that it allows a pondering writer like me to explore *possibilities*. So Hunter's story is just that: a fictional exploration of one possibility.

I actually had a few false starts on this novel—a common but not necessarily unhappy part of the process. And then I think I was riding my bike to the beach one day and, in true Hollywood fashion, the proverbial clouds parted and wham! I saw the big granite rock and knew that's where the story would get going. All I had to do, so to speak, was make the leap along with Hunter.

Sometimes it looks as if Hunter is completely at the mercy of forces he cannot control—for example, by the "committees" that are in charge of heaven. Yet at other times, it's Hunter's will that gets him into and out of trouble. In the end, is Hunter in charge of his own fate?

We are all at the mercy of many forces we cannot control and we must live with that reality, no matter how kind or unkind it might be. But we feel obliged, in small ways and sometimes big ways, to assert our free will, to make a stand, to take a big gamble, to charge off into the unknown and see what happens. Sometimes we make a difference. Sometimes we discover our limitations. Sometimes we make a big mistake. But every time we dare to "disturb the universe," we feel more fully alive. Like Hunter, we are not fully in charge of our fate—in this life or whatever comes after. But we must assert our will in some way and it can make some kind of difference in the larger fabric of life. Hunter does want to make a difference, but since he can never (like us) fully comprehend the big picture, he is prone to make mistakes—even doing harm while trying to do good.

The whole scheme of free will versus predestination is eternally puzzling and frustrating, yet the story reflects the need in all of us to act—and sometimes act decisively and dramatically—rather than let events control us.

What appealed to you about the character of Archie, as you were planning the story?

Archie is a kind of guru/mentor, and possibly a trickster, who has his own unique personality and style. The question is whether he is reliable or not, or whether he even really knows what's going on (in heaven and elsewhere). He has a kind of charming ambiguity and good nature, but also admits that there is no such thing as complete knowledge. In some ways, he is a manifestation of God but certainly not the God of the Old Testament. He is amiable and caring and is trying to do the best he can for the newly arrived. He guides the recently deceased and he coaches Hunter to be a guide of sorts—providing what is needed to make incoming souls comfortable in the new and ever-shifting world of heaven.

What appeals to you about the verse novel format as a way to tell a story?

It's a playful novel in some ways, although dead serious in many others. The verse form is also rather playful and it's also visual. It allows me to create a unique rhythm of words and emphasis on certain ideas and contrasting ideas.

I think the reading experience is radically different from a prose novel and the form invites the reader to linger a bit on the page or, if they choose, to read the whole story fairly quickly—and then maybe revisit it sometime later to enjoy the structure and sound as well as the content.

In this novel, you're playing with language, ideas, characters. At the same time, you have created a set of characters we care about. What are the challenges in achieving that balance?

Dealing with such a deeply significant topic as life/death/afterlife is fraught with many pitfalls. A heavy-handed approach could be quite dreadful, so I tried to make sure the characters themselves were very human, flawed, vulnerable, and somewhat naïve. As we all contemplate our own mortality, those are characteristics we all share. Hunter is young and ill-prepared for his own death and what comes after, but since he has no deep seated religious beliefs or fatalistic attitude, he's rather open to whatever comes next. He has trouble figuring out the how's and why's of the new set of rules about how life/death/afterlife works, but he finds it fascinating and has an open mind.

In that regard, there's something gently Kafkaesque about the story. Maybe there are no hard and fast rules about anything. (And, of course, maybe the afterlife we experience is greatly of our own creation, aided by God or spirit or universe or whatever.)

Trinity is a truly wounded individual that Hunter wants to help. He reminds me that when we encounter deeply damaged people at points in our lives, we should do the best to help them if we possibly can. So I guess it's Hunter's compassion that helps carry the story.

How important is it for you as a storyteller to indulge in "play" as you develop a story and characters?

Play was very important here. At first, my rule was that there was no rule. I let Hunter and the story take me down some intriguing and amazing paths to see where it led. This, of course, got me into a tangled jungle of possibilities and I got lost. Getting lost is half the fun of a good adventure. So I had to untangle things, bring some order to the chaos without losing the energy that healthy chaos brings to fiction. I had no idea how the story would end or if a real hard-landing ending was even appropriate. As usual, my protagonist insisted on where the tale needed to go and guided me out of the messy, exotic wilderness and into the light.

Among other things, it's pretty nervy of you to play with the idea of "heaven." What appealed to you about that challenge as you created this story?

Like many, I guess I would have considered (and possibly believed) our many variations of what heaven can be:
a) perfect, beautiful world of light and leisure
b) some place much like earth but where only good things happen
c) communion with a paternal God who tells you the secrets of the universe
d) a waystation to sort out a few things before being reincarnated
e) a purely spiritual place with no need for any physical dimension
f) pure consciousness.

That's the short list, I suppose. I guess the fact that no one has ever nailed down exactly what happens to us when we die keeps us intrigued, confused, inspired, and curious. Fiction is such a great vehicle to explore possibilities without being certain or preachy that I couldn't help myself. I would certainly love to hear from anyone within the spiritual realm (or living, for that matter) who could provide more insight into the great mystery of what comes next when our life comes to a close. Please feel free to contact me telepathically or at lesleychoyce@yahoo.com

Thank you, Lesley.